C U Next Tuesday

A cacophony of chatter, laughter and sounds of glasses clinking, blended and fused into static silence. Ice in his glass and on his teeth evoked memories of being carried on his father's shoulders along Ballymoney beach and the click-clacking of the stones. They always walked to the shipwreck. What was once the site of a tragedy had become, for him, hallowed ground where wisdom was imparted. The vessel that had left Liverpool for Rio de Janeiro was now rusting away off the Wexford coast. All of the crew was lost. A tragic waste of life... like there in the smoking area, he thought.

Although surrounded by friends and substitutes for friends, he was detached and distracted. His cheerless eyes averted from the scene encompassing him and downturned into his pint. He didn't want to be there but he definitely didn't want to stay at home wallowing alone. If he drank enough his cheekbones would rise, his expectations would fall, certainly his standards would plummet, and perhaps he would laugh and smile if only for a while. Then the night could fizzle out and he could return home to dreamless sleep.

The smoking area was packed on this Tuesday night, a weekly student hip-hop night appropriately named *Cunt*. (C.U. Next Tuesday) Guys in skinny-jeans and V-necked t-shirts posed exposing hairless chests. He had felt self-conscious and out of place in his faded decade-old Nine Inch Nails t-shirt but the obviousness of this juxtaposition went unnoticed amidst the metrosexual milieu preoccupied with the flurry of indie chicks in disco pants, smoking with airs of indifference, expressionless, hips popped. He recalled a recently erected Facebook community called *"You're Not Indie,*

You're Just a Dope in a Granny Jumper". He surveyed the smoking area noting several such stereotypes being perpetuated. His initial amusement was brief; his feelings of derision turning to feelings of guilt for his own bitterness realising how clichéd his contempt was, recalling his own sense of "style" and cavalier attitude at twenty.

Guys' eyes groped the girls entering from the parapet above, smirks and glances exchanged affirming their unanimous opinions. He viewed a group of recognisables on the other side of the pit and envisaged a stream of events that might likely occur on that or any other of their nights.

At the rate they were drinking, even if any of them did manage to take someone home, whisky-dick would present itself coupled with a full bladder and the ever-present anti-foreplay chitchat of "I don't usually do this kind of thing" or any variation of an erection eradicating epilogue precluding progress, only then for her to dry-hump for a period before whispering with pukey-smokey breath, "Do you have a condom?" expecting him at full-mast instantaneously at the sight of her tactless attempt at striptease, followed by the cupping of his then receding balls with chipped nail-varnished claws. With considerable effort on her part, orally, she will have roused a slidable condomless semi, suitable for some semblance of stationery missionary, prior to the sensible but really just scared-shitless-of-procreating-with-this-creature, practice of coitous-interruptus. Morning would come as would the smell of stale sweat and her unsubtle soliloquy jokingly-seriously expressing her plea that he not "go around bragging to all his mates". Neither will have cum and all he'd want is her to leave. Awkward tea and toast or a bottle of Lucozade and a hoodie he'd never see again.

In reporting back to his mates he would speak of the sex, as men who have taken part in such sex always do, that is to say, as they would have liked it to have been and as they have heard it described by others. He'd open his story with a modest introduction with the intention of telling things exactly as they happened as well as he could, booze being a factor, but imperceptibly, and inevitably, he would pass into falsehood. "Lashed her out-of-it" he'd say. Confining oneself to the facts in instances such as these is difficult and cunts of that ilk, he thought, were rarely capable of it.

*

What occurred to him was that the best case scenario would be if he was to, at some point over the course of the night, get chatting to some temperate soubrette undeserving of the same scorn as others present. They could chat conscientiously about the state of the nation, the state of their mates, and warm to one another in their shared sentiments and finally exchange a wholesome parting kiss. They would have vocalised their shared contempt for the "three-day rule" and the prescribed societal gender roles. To demonstrate their opposition to this *she* would call him the following afternoon to meet for a coffee and a walk by the canal to observe the ducks and swans. That wouldn't be a complete fucking waste of time, he thought.

What was more likely was that this appealing figure would not emerge and he would leave close to half-two so as to avoid the last-chance chancers of mates of his trying it on, trying his patience, only then to not make haste on their assured trip for food, queuing in the cold, periodically being pecked at by the queue-encircling smoke-scabbers. A taxi home alone with a preemptive disclosure to the driver assuring him that courtesy would be shown and he'd be spared the "Busy night tonight?" chitchat…to which the driver

would express his thanks genuinely in word and gesture with a "Cheers", turning up *Newstalk*, not taking the scenic route, and delivering his passenger home safely without subjecting him to any archaic anecdotal advice or insight into his prejudices. The knowledge of his eventual escape was not comforting. The night was young.

Logic had quashed the idea that his life was entirely hopeless. Suicide was too dramatic, too final and too hurtful to others. He hadn't felt empty with her. He missed the togetherness. He missed the laughter. He missed the shared experiences. He missed the mutual understanding of one another. He knew that he could have that again with someone but it had been three years. He'd had some short-term "wool-sweater" relationships but he'd felt nothing acutely. However, what's said is often true, it's only when you stop looking...

*

As she descended the steps he looked-on frozen in anticipation. Her pale white cheeks were visible, framed by her winered hair. Her eyes were veiled by the downturned brim of her domed black hat. A black cloak hugged her petite frame. From head to toe she was perfection in his eyes. A long black velvet dress barely exposed her feet, clad in black suede boots, laced all the way to the knee or higher, covering what he could only presume to be fishnets. The light shone off a ring she was wearing which bore a symbol he recognised. Two half-moons facing east and west separated and connected by a full circle, the Wiccan symbol for goddess. Her prominent chin and nose combined with everything else about her aesthetic left only a broomstick missing. If a girl could make him cry and feel, she was worth knowing. She looked capable.

She slid away to a vacant space, drew out and lit a cigarette. With candor she sipped from a stainless steel hipflask before placing it back in her bag. Checking her phone she looked at it expressionlessly and scrolled before holding down her thumb, appearing to turn it off and beckoned a friend to come to her. She said something confidently before dropping the phone into her friend's bag. That kind of display of logic and self-control confirmed the strength he had already assumed her to have. Her apparent ability to detach herself so coolly from some ostensible annoyance in her life pleased him greatly. Enthralled, he looked on.

Her chin rose slowly and her darkshadowed eyes surveyed the area gradually, her face unmoving, seemingly as unimpressed as he by their surroundings, and with equal measures of revulsion and apathy, they drew out another smoke each, in unison, apart.

He began to daydream imagining himself with her, his head in her lap as she read to him the sonnets of Shakespeare, the happy hunting ground for his mind when it had lost its balance.

She was the type of girl who was frugal, searching charity shops, adorning herself with what others had strewn aside, delineating a grace and elegance all her own. She was the type of girl who loved the smell of old books, which she would read alone in her cold studio apartment, warming herself with peppermint tea. She was the type of girl who loved silent films and had collections of risqué French wartime postcards. She was the type of girl who enjoyed her own company. She was the type of girl who had few close friends but those she had were highly valued. She was the type of girl who could not tell a lie. She was happy to be misunderstood. She was the type of girl who would rather be hated for what she was, than be loved for what she was not. She was not opinionated but certainly held strong opinions, educated by her life's experience, leaving no room for conjecture. She was the type of girl who had passion. She was defiant, decisive, devoted, self-reliant, punctual, and unselfish. She was artistic and ambitious. She was conscientious, candid, and clever. She was an individual. She was damaged. She had been and was now being mistreated by someone beneath her. She could sew and repair garments but had been unable to fix or save the guys she'd been with in the past. She didn't need anyone else, nor did he, but their kind were better partnered than alone. He pictured himself refilling her wine glass, she in the bath, makeupless, happy, giving him a smile with a future in it.

For a college project some years before, he had done a painting of his ideal woman and coupled it with an appropriate song with the lyrics, "I miss you...But I haven't met you yet" by Bjork. He'd never seen this girl before but he'd painted her portrait.

He imagined that if an advance were to be welcomed by her it would have to be tactful, unthreatening, and above all else, sober. He wasn't too drunk yet, however if he was to be, he may very well botch what chance he might have had in making a good first impression.

*

Inside nothing was more sobering to him than the cavalcade of cool-kids from Dublin suburbs cavorting semi-comfortably to a choral a cappella of Jay-Z building up to a song, holding poses, pointing to friends, conjuring up spurious hip-hop styled stances, arms folded, lips pursed, eyes scrunched closed in painful anticipation of the beat dropping...The familiar sound of heavy-flowing urine hitting toilet water, coupled with the sound of sleigh bells ringing reverberated from the speakers, "Gin & Juice" by Snoop Dogg. Most people present were born around the time that record came out but nonetheless were mouthing the lyrics word-perfect, harmoniously. The projector screen behind the DJ's booth was showing snippets from *White Men Can't Jump* and alternated montages of photos of previous nights at *Cunt*. Every time a picture featured someone present, cheers erupted.

The dance floor filled so he had a place to sit and sober. Raising his cup of orange juice he saluted his friends, who judging by their enthusiastic responses, assumed him to be drinking gin and juice in honour of the song playing. The DJ veered off into an obscure song by Eazy-E, half-emptying the floor notwithstanding his fist pumping and crooning of the lyrics earnestly.

His mates beckoned him follow as they moved into the next room. He did. As he reached the threshold between rooms he could see her hugging a friend of hers. Her smile made his chest warm. As the embrace ended and she withdrew he noticed tattoos on the insides of her arms. One arm bore heart with a keyhole and the other an antique styled key. She then proceeded in gathering her stuff and walked towards the exit. This development put him in a momentary state of panic. His chest tightened and he felt pain. Would he get another chance to see her, under better circumstances? Would he ever see her again, period?

His initial plan of getting drunk enough to have a good time was reinstated. His lowered inhibitions led to partaking in generalised revelry for the next few hours. As the night drew to a close the lights came up languidly lighting the room. He, jacketless, re-entered the smoking area while his friends were herded by bouncers into the coat- check line.

FUCK...

She was still there, back in the smoking area alone, checking her phone. She too, appeared to be waiting for her friends.

He began to assume a sober demeanor.

A drunk French guy sitting at a table close to her, spoke *at* her swaying, apologising for his English not being very good. Several extensions of his arm offering a smoke were politely declined.

A potential avenue to appeal to her occurred to him. If he could distract the French guy and gain some eye contact with her and give her a look of sympathy, perhaps she'd smile and mouth a "thanks".
        "Excusez-moi; Tu peux me donner du feu?" An expression of amazement came across the French guy's face whose hand involuntarily became displaced from her shoulder and then flowed and wafted with his other hand in rhapsodic gesture as he spoke. "Tu parles français?" "No not really...Merci mille fois". In his periphery he became painfully aware by her continued nonresponsive statuesque mien, that she either was not paying any attention to his attempted genteel gallantry or was fully aware of what he was playing-at and was not impressed. "A votre santé!" and with that the French guy saw some friends and ambled on. Her head reclined slightly so that she could look at him out from under the brim of her hat and smiled almost conceitedly, suggesting some thanks and at the same time, bidding him fuck off. Before he could graciously leave her with a "have a good night", her friend appeared and in an instant she was gone, leaving him with nothing but a beautiful image, beguiled and feeling bitter loss.

Alonewardbound with his box of smokes an empty vessel and lighter lost or pocketed, he feared for the worst which was, at this juncture, the arduous task of trying to get to sleep without relief. With his body too drunk and drained to manually accomplish a nocturnal emission or any smokes to lighten his head, he feared for the rolls, tosses and turns.

As though a merciful and clairvoyant *Watcher* had flown ahead to spare him this plight, he found a single cigarette and a box of matches awaiting him on his windowsill. He gave thanks, poked his head out of his bedroom window and looked for her. He sparked, sucked deep, exhaled and calmed. Becoming lightheaded with the smoke dwindling, he crushed the cigarette into the window's ledge, likening the embers to his hopes that dispersed into the thick black night, knowing he would dream of her.

Aurora Borealis

The men's bathroom door slowly closed after a fleeing punter, dampening out the sound of thumping music. Baz could only ever piss in an even-flow when he was alone. Although the cubicle was unoccupied, he was deterred by shivering pools on the floor and the brown-stained wad lagooning in the overflowing bowl. At the middle urinal, he leaned forward pressing his forehead against the wall and peered curiously at what he likened to planetary orbit; one enormous neon-yellow deodorizing block, surrounded by others both blue and pink, of varying weathered sizes. Which of them was Earth?

The pill he had taken earlier was beginning to loosen his mind, which up until that point, had been occupied by the inaccuracies in his pay slip, his failing relationship, and more prominently, the cancerous tumours spreading through his mother's breasts.

This was the first night he'd ever imbibed any chemicals. The course of treatment however was highly advisable considering his grief-stricken state, his mate had implored.

A dull tapping from the music beyond, reached him through the wall, reverberating through his skull. He felt calm, almost alone. The muscles in his body limbered. His piss released in unison with the water gushing from the urinal. The eroded deodorizing blocks were raised up by the water and swirled frantically around the seemingly immovable yellow orb in the centre. How long does it take for each planet to orbit the sun he thought? Perhaps it looks this fast in the eyes of God?

He approached the mirror and with his pelvis pressed against the counter, leaned-in, and stared into the vast dilated darkness in his then tranquil eyes. He rolled up his sleeves and gave thanks. While washing his hands, frosty foam rolled over his bloodless knuckles, white maned horses, escaping into the abyss of the unguarded drain. The bathroom attendant, all smiles, ripped him off three generous sheets of blue paper towel. In the mirror he noticed the three urinals protruding from the white-tiled wall, taking form. Life beginning in all its glory. He now saw these ovals as radiant pregnant bellies; three generations. Two were the same height. The last was aged, marred, and plaster had been applied to hide the crack that scarred it. The middle one looked less worn and its porcelain whiteness made it stand out more in the blinking florescent light. Its side was tattooed with black permanent marker; a beauty by all accounts. The last one was lower, still a child, the granddaughter.

He no longer felt the agitating noise. He felt peace. He could die there and then gratefully. All comes full circle. He'd be gone but these seven folks or more would remain and furthermore, go forth to flush... flourish.

He was just finishing patting down his hands when the door slammed open and two men came barging in, rushing towards the urinals, unzipping their jeans. The older of the two was in his late twenties but looked forty. He was short and fat. He let-loose a heavy stream, his fist pounding against the wall in relief. "Jayzus!" The younger of the two was maybe twenty and looked it. He was wide-eyed, tall and skinny. They adhered to proper pissing-etiquette and left a space between them. The younger of the pair tightened and released his grip, conducting his flow in a sensible stream whilst letting out a delicate sigh of relief without any theatrics.

The elder gave a careless shake, zipped-up and turned exposing droplets of stray piss on his faded blue jeans and tanned boots while snarling at the youth. "C'mon for fuck sake, we don't have all bleedin night!" In response, a little slurredly, "Here, wud-jew relaaax the cax ye moany cunt...I'm taken me time". With that, the elder turned in a strop and marched towards the counter and coughed up a glob of green phlegm into the sink, his shameless mouth dribbling and eyes glazing, before brushing past the attendant, "Sorry Sambo, I've no change pal".

A seed of malice, Baz felt, had been sewn.

Baz slid his hands into his pockets as the young pisser was finishing, who turned towards him and the attendant, offering a "Schtory' boyez" before flipping a 50 cent piece into the ashtray and sauntering out the still-closing door through the music coming from outside and to the music in his head.

Silver encircled gold. A shimmering two-Euro coin had arisen coupled with a few coppers and a 10 cent piece, from the depths of the lint-laden pockets of Baz. He blew rinds of tobacco off the coins and watched them cascade towards the brown-tiled floor. He placed the coins in the ashtray provided and peered deeply into the welcoming eyes of the attendant. Baz initiated a two-handed clasping handshake and closed his stinging eyes and shook with an almost ceremonious sincerity. He felt the warmth from the coarse strong hand that squeezed back and listened to the soft words

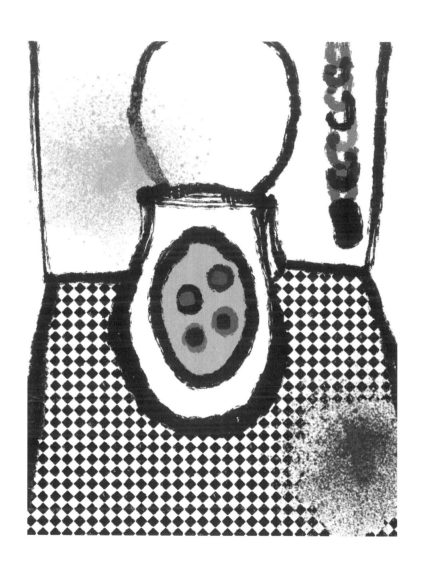

carried on a minty breeze, "Av a good night my friend and God bless you". Baz released his grip and in opening his eyes, exposed his black-stone pupils to the attendant. Baz ground his teeth then licked his lips and slowly shaking his head said, in what he thought a cool and stoic manner, "No man...Thank You...You're a good man. Cheers." And with that he gave the attendant a brief dramatic hug, inhaling deeply the Versace, before snagging a lemon-lolly and heading for the door. "Ok my friend, you av' a good night ok...taek' good kay-ah of you-ah-sell". As Baz walked towards the closed door, the African accent echoed in his mind and blossomed into a flurry of thought. The door bore a mounted mirror and Baz idealized the attendant, majestic, perched upon his barstool throne, behind him. He thought of the wisdom of MUFASA!

"Simba...Everything you see exists together in a delicate balance. You need to understand that balance, and respect all the creatures from the crawling ant to the leaping antelope."

The images that had flashed in Baz' mind of smashing in the face of the Phlegmer with the empty ashtray that would have fitted perfectly into the palm of his hand, ceased, and were replaced by those adorable lion-cubs play-fighting, in joyful reverie. He and the Phlegmer as friends perhaps?

"We are all connected in the great circle of life".

The Phlegmer was loved by someone somewhere and he too had loved, surely? We've all felt pain, been wronged and done wrong, Baz thought.

"When we die our bodies become the grass and the antelope eat the grass. We are all connected in the great circle of life".

Baz' insignificance in the grand scheme of things comforted him as did the Phlegmer's. This knowledge washed over him in an awesome wave of heat and light. Looking in the mirror he barely recognised himself. Who he was did not matter. One day he would be grass.

*

House music had never been too his taste. He'd never gotten-it before but the pill had allowed it in and the music had taken-hold, swaying his body back and forth in a tide of sound. A sea of hands moved in rhapsodic gesture, poses frozen, flickering rapidly in the strobe light. Sixty portraits per second. Speaking in tongues, the revelers ritualistically mouthed whatever lyrics made sense to them in murmurs of newly created languages, releasing demons from their sanctified mouths. He beheld the beautiful people, all now joined in ordination. He felt their souls amalgamating in the cloud of illuminated fog, emanating from tabernacle-esque boxes upon the DJ's altar. The ceiling disappeared and he could see the northern lights. The pleasure centers in his brain simultaneously lit-up the same colours as the sky.

Later he found himself hugging a speaker, its gusting air cooling his sweat-crowned brow. He was charging on this hub and the musical energy radiating assimilated into his system. It coursed through his veins and pounding heart, which, if it were to fail, surely would be restarted instantly to function at a higher capacity given the presence of this divine current.

On his way through the crowd towards the smoking area, an encounter with a friendly-faced stranger gave occasion for exchanges of good wishes, heart-felt hugs, and fearless flattery of each other's exquisiteness. They held each other, chests pressed tight, their hearts beating palpably in harmony. As their hug ended and their faces parted, some of her hair clung to his face, hanging like vines from the mystical forest of her head. Some of his little people could swing through the vines and stay with her and vice versa. "I FUCKING LOVE YOUR HAIR" he said "IT'S LIKE... IT'S LIKE RUMPLESTILLSKIN SPUN GOLD THREAD, AND THAT'S YOUR HAIR!" With that she removed her keys and using an unfolded sewing scissors, cut off a lock, placed it in his open palm, then closed it tight. She pulled his face close to hers and after running her thick moist tongue up his cheek, sucked on his earlobe, before yelling, "DON'T SPEND IT ALL IN ONE GO!" In parting, a blessing was given, in the form of the sign of the cross, being licked onto her glistening forehead. "WHAT'S YOUR NAME?" he shouted as she was backing away. "I ACTUALLY DON'T EVEN KNOW ANYMORE!" she replied, before turning, smiling and walking back onto the dance floor. Lycra clung to her athletic frame and he watched in awe, the hypnotic pendulum of her firm buttocks rise and fall with each parting step.

He had been blessed and felt it only right forever more to live out his days doing good deeds. A double vodka and Red Bull, cashback and tokens for the cigarette machine were what was called for and he was on his merry way. Outside he unveiled a holy trinity: a pack of John Player Blue, a pack Marlboro Gold and a pack of Camel Blue. Baz crusaded through the cold, dispensing offerings to all those in need.

He noticed the Phlegmer standing solo, shivering, and searching his pockets. An opportunity to extend the hand of friendship had presented itself.

The Phlegmer welcomed this advance, their pupils mirroring, and when the subject of chemicals came up, Baz disclosed that it was his first time. The Phlegmer felt compelled to dispel any anxiety that his newfound friend might have by presenting him with comforting facts.

"It's just silly man, that these yokes are illegal. The fucking powers that be...That's the real craic at play. Evil empire and that. It's not dangerous to us but a danger to government's revenue ye know? They'd rather us get gee-eyed and tax the bollox off us. And what does that legal substance do... yeah? Us killing each other after a few scoops; the passive aggression sweeping up through us...bloody murder on drink. No one smoking a sneaky joint ever went out and kicked some defenseless cunt to death did they? And these? These beautiful pills man...What do they do? Make you dance and smile and love the world...Love each other...Love the people you hated yesterday...Love yourself even? Singing "WE ARE YOUR FRIENDS" and all "YOU'LL NEVER BE ALONE AGAIN" and all that, d'ye know what I mean like? Soundest buzz ever, no animosity or nothing. Sure it was a feckin Catholic priest who was one of its biggest advocates, saying it opened up his only ever genuine dialogue with God for fuck sake; said it was like bleedin being Moses on the mountain, having revelations and all, never feeling more connected to yer man upstairs! What the fuck is wrong with that? Peace on earth? The Church maybe is the answer; one priest to fuck up your life and then another to give you this rebirth, making you whole again...It was developed as medication for fuck sake, treating cunts suffering from PTSD and terminally ill cunts on the shittest buzz ever, making them feel less shit ye know? And here, in this economic climate and with the price of drink, a shrewd and frugal gent such as myself needs to make choices! I'll have a Camel Blue man, cheers..... Few of these yips and on the water all night, then a brisk walk home to cool down, as opposed to spending a fucking bomb on drink and then a taxi home cause you're legless or dare I fuckin say, the horrors on the cunting Nitelink?...FUCK THAT! Then that geebag Nancy Reagan on her Just Say No lark and the rest of those shower of scumbags got it criminalised as part of their own poxy conservative agenda so that now every cunt out there is making it BUT cutting it with a load of shite...That's why young fellas end up dead...It's not the MDMA man. Look, prescription meds kill fuckin loads more people than the odd dodgy pill...And here, this won't come as a shock to you man, I'm sure, but those bastards committed a fucking crime in the first place, making it illegal by doing a fake study that later had to go on to be recanted n'all coz it was a load of bollox! Those scumbags had whole campaigns n'all saying even just one yoke can give you Parkinson's for fuck sake! Drink a load of water and you'll be fuckin grand, and don't take anything else or smoke any weed because you'll be all over the kip... And just don't have anything to do the next day and recuperate in a nice positive atmosphere with people who are sound like... I've to leg it over here man but keep-it-real, and here, thanks for the smoke; you're a gent! I've got a little present for you too. To new found brethren whah? METH-LENE-DIOXY-METH-AMPHETA-Ah-here-what's-MEAN- and what's mine is yours... Take one for later or whenever. Pills Like White Elephants as yer man once said... Talk-te-ye, I'm leggin-it, G'luck".

*

Baz walked past the que of bobbing taxis outside to venture by foot and air, taking heed of the advice from the elder Phlegmer. After giving his coat to a young lad sat on the Ha'penny Bridge and the remaining smokes, he soldiered on to his girlfriend's apartment a little further down the quays. Looking up at her window, he imagined what her night most likely consisted of; the painstaking task of lesson-planning and dealing with a finicky laminating machine, imortalising her junior infants Easter art. Disturbing her was out of the question. She had to wake up in two hours. No.

His mother might not wake up at all, he thought. Tears filled his eyes. He walked and kept on walking, vigorously inhaling through his nose and breathing out his mouth for the miles that lay ahead, as he'd done when running cross-country, all those years ago.

*

As he reached the driveway he could see the flickering T.V. light pulsating on the curtains of his mother's bedroom window. She hadn't been sleeping well, or at all, ever since her diagnosis. He quietly let himself in and made tea for two. After lightly tapping on her bedroom door he was sweetly beckoned in.

Without a word she greeted him with a warm smile and turned off the news as he placed her favourite mug on the bedside locker. "Silence like a cancer grows" he said, winking and smiling, while removing her Simon and Garfunkel record from its sleeve, which had been atop a stack of likewise melancholic vinyl. "It's great how we can talk like this...everyone tip-toeing around it is driving me crazy" she said smiling, and regarded him through tired mothers' eyes. She sipped her tea.

"There are a few things you need to know", he said. "You don't need to be afraid. You are a good person. I'm going to tell you the same thing I told Dad before... There's no need for fear, at all. Not everybody shares your faith, but it should be a comfort to you now. If you truly believe what you've been preaching to me for years... There's no need for any fear. A better place, right? Our time on this earth is but a pin-prick in eternity, No? Death be not proud, and all that? You have had a joyous life, right? You've always been happy and proud of all you and Dad achieved and how you raised us. You had a great life and a pretty fucking great partner too. We have the best relationship of anyone I know, and you just need to know that I am your friend and you'll never be alone..."

Tears filled her eyes. "I know, Love. I'm so proud of you... Now go and get some feckin sleep you lunatic. Thanks for the tea."

"Listen. You need to sleep too. You need to close your eyes and drift away from all this horror on the screen. Then tomorrow, you'll have the energy to run, like you always have, and feel good. Get that Dopamine and Serotonin going, yeah? Better pass boldly into that other world in the glory of your passion, than wither dismally the fuck away here right? I'll go for a run with you if you like..."

He dimmed the lights and kissed her closing eyes goodnight.

*

Sophie, the cat, surfaced from a clothes basket in the utility room and padded her way into the living room where Baz lay on the floor in front of the fire, bollock naked. The glow from an open laptop's face cast him in white light giving him a ghostlike complexion and Sophie hissed before lying down beside him. He was making a playlist for his mother, to run to, comprised of all the songs he knew she loved. He looked into Sophie's guileless eyes observing him judiciously. Baz felt as though he could be looking into the eyes of God.

He was coming down as the sun was coming up but sleep was out of the question. He wanted to be able to spend the day with his mother and make her happy. He half-contemplated putting the remaining pill in her coffee later that morning when she rose. If only she could feel what he'd felt, euphoria.

Sunlight began breaking through the gap in the curtains. The shard in Sophie's line of vision prompted her to move, scaling the bookcase with a baffling degree of agility. Sophie scrutinised Baz' fingers as they tapped away at the keys.

He thought about the junkies on the streets and kids starving in Africa. He thought about the poor bathroom attendant subjected to breathing in the pathogens from the deodorizing urinal blocks night after night. He thought about his father.

Rolling over onto his back he stared up and began to ask Sophie philosophical questions about the meaning of existence, the relativity of time and, respectfully, queried the cause of her cruelty? Why did she allow bad things to happen to good people? Sophie considered these questions whilst licking her paws but she did not answer. Baz carried on dragging and dropping songs by Blondie and Annie Lennox and the next time he rolled over to ask Sophie up in the sky a question, she was gone.

He sat upright and searched his pockets. Opening his palm in a mystified gaze, he examined the tiny speckled pill.

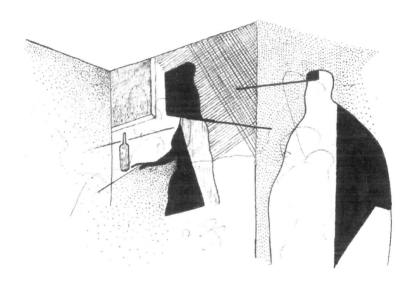

Stemless Wine Glasses

She opened the door and said nothing. Before he had a chance to look her in the eyes and say he was sorry, she turned her back on him and slid through the cold unlit hall. He likened the sound of her slippers creasing the carpet to that of crunching snow. The porthole of light she'd gone through was narrowing behind her as the door into the living room clicked closed. Shadows crept over a line of photo frames, the smiling faces vanishing into darkness. The last thing he saw was his keys hanging up, just where he'd left them.

His eyes stung as he carelessly hit the lights and instantly regretting this, applied an appropriate amount of rotation to the dimmer, leaving him with just enough light to make it through the hall without knocking anything over. Passing the pictures of the holidays abroad, he was not transported, but stopped for a moment starring at the last one. The photo he'd knocked off the wall and broken a few days prior had been replaced with another. He knew by the Spanish football jerseys that the picture must have been during the World Cup, on their last stop on the way home from travelling; Santiago de Compostela. Her hands were clasped around his waist, chin resting on his shoulder, her long blonde hair framing a sun-kissed, smiling, freckled face. Looking at the two happy people in focus, he wondered to himself, what the fuck had happened?

He entered the room and the pungent aroma of the Sun & Sand Yankee candle hit him. He controlled his gag reflex by exhaling harshly out his nose. The initially blurry television screen became clear; Cormac from *Tallaghtfornia's* paused face filled the muted screen. The sound of the cutlery drawer closing brought his attention around the partition, into the kitchen. The popping sound of the cork sent shivers down his spine and prompted him to say that he was "alright for one", but this comment was met with raised eyebrows and a bemused vacant stare that suggested to him that she didn't give a fuck what he wanted, and that the uncorked bottle was for her. This deduction was confirmed as she closed the press and placed down on the counter beside the bottle of *Alvariño*, a single stemless wineglass.

Sorry I for forgot-

Your keys? Yeah well, what's new? I wouldn't give a fuck if it was the weekend but some of us actually have real jobs and need to be up in the morning.

Yeah I know I'm a fucking-

Eh, retard? Yeah I know...what do you want to drink?

Honestly, I'm just a bit-

Yeah, I know...Pissed, but that's never stopped you before.

I'll just grab a-

You finished it. There's no Whiskey.

Grand, I'll just have a-

There's no beers. Kate was over earlier and we had the last two. I told you to pick some up remember...

Sorry I forgot, I was just out with-

Shut up will you...and just get a drink; I don't give a shit who you were with. Anyone you were out with this late on a fucking Tuesday can't be anyone who's not a total loser.

With that she brushed past him and sat down on the couch. He opened the press and scanning both shelves, swallowed the lump in his throat, seeing only coffee mugs and her stemless wineglasses. She heard the press door being opened and grinding her teeth, imagined the stupid look on his face.

Do we not have any-

No, we don't...We have one left that has a stem, given that you've broken ALL the others and it's in the wash...

Starring resentfully at the stemless glasses, he took one and walked into the living room.

This is my *Alvariño*, there's some other stuff in the fridge.

He opened the fridge seeing bottles of *Pinot Grigio* and *Sauvignon Blanc*. He drank *Chardonnay*, if he had to. She'd obviously done a shop given that the fridge was fully stocked, the meats, dairy, veg, and assorted items being in their appropriate place and all the condiments' labels faced outward. He slid the bottle out along with a bunch of white seedless grapes.

For fuck sake, don't uncork that unless you plan on drinking the whole bottle. Drink the *Pinot Grigio*...the one with the twist-off cap.

Yes I am going to drink the whole bottle you cunt. (He thought to himself)

And don't start eating those grapes either. We're having Eoin and Sarah over tomorrow, or did you forget?

Walking back into the kitchen he called back saying "No I didn't forget, but I was talking to Eoin tonight and he said he might not be able to make it...(Waiting for a response)...he said he may get called in to the bar if no one else can cover for Dave but that he'd-

Well that makes no difference because Sarah is coming and so are John and Ann. Please do NOT eat the grapes...Or the cheese, please.

He took a deep breath, and in unison with the closing fridge door, sighed, before returning to living room, and lay his head in her lap. Her pout softened into a smile as she looked into his tired eyes and said, "You're some feckin eejit".

She put on a DVD, *Meet the Parents*. This perhaps was her attempt at a peace offering he thought, as it was a shared love of theirs. She skipped forward to the first scene with the parents. "I can't believe no one ever told you that you're the spit of Robert De Niro. The faces you pull and even the mole...and the butt-chin!" She squeezed his chin into a more pronounced arse-shape with her thumb and index finger and with her other hand, pinched his cheeks to make his mouth move while she ventriloquized, "Have you ever watched pornographic videos Greg?" and swirling an almost empty glass, "Here, will you top me up? Open whatever one you want". He rose and walked to the humming fridge and feared for what lay ahead.

*

Three and a half bottles of wine later and they were both well and truly in a heap.

The DVD menu was looping with the same sounds repeating every twenty seconds or so. The image of Ben Stiller hooked up to the lie-detector machine and De Niro's face, his face, scrutinized Stiller's. He might have looked like De Niro but as of late, he felt like Stiller, constantly under surveillance, resented, and thought of as not being good enough, for her anyway, the successful fashion Buyer.

He carried her to bed and both fully clothed, passed out.

*

Soon he felt the sun on his face and the sound of birds chirping allowed him to recall what he had hidden in his guitar case. She had mentioned more than once in the last week that she'd meant to pick up another bird feeder. Despite her apparent aversion to him and most people in general, one of her more human qualities was a genuine love of all animals. Nothing pleased her more than to sit sipping tea while watching birds on the balcony. He'd read the paper and pretend not to notice her smiling.

She was still fast asleep, frowning, and periodically muttered something about "deadlines". He sat upright slowly and got out of bed cautiously so as to not rouse her. He tiptoed into the living room and delicately opened his creaking case. He removed the hidden birdfeeder and holding his breath, slowly inched open the sliding door, just enough to sidestep through. He hung the birdfeeder from the hook he'd put up ages ago and removed one of the several (due to always forgetting one) tiny locks he'd gotten in the gym, to secure the it, so that it would not be knocked off and taken like the last one, by whom she suspected to be the "fucking magpie bastards". He hadn't been thoughtful enough to close the sliding door behind himself. He'd only accounted for the sound the door might make in sliding closed but neglected to consider the draft that was making its way through their cracked bedroom door. The backdraft jingled her jewelry hanging from hooks above her bedside locker. Startled, she jumped up in bed and just as she did, heard the living room door slam with the draft. Rage swept up through her torso.

I'm going to fucking kill him. I'm going to fucking kill him, the LYING, SNEAKY, CUNT!

She marched through the hall and the pounding of her feet alerted him to her imminent arrival and put him in a momentary state of shock. He'd been so quiet, he thought. Images of their past flickered in his mind. Later he'd draw comparisons of this moment to what he'd imagined a near death experience would be like, life flashing before one's eyes.

ARE YOU FUCKIN SERIOUS YOU ABSOLUTE BASTARD, CREEPING AROUND LIKE A FUCKING CHILD!

He opened his mouth to draw breath. His throat was dry and his legs shivered in the cold. No words came and she continued.

I'M A FUCKING FOOL...YOU PROMISED ME YOU WOULDN'T SMOKE HERE. YOU'RE A FUCKING LOSER.

They'd initially tried quitting together and she'd had some success. The compromise was that if he was unable to quite completely, that he wouldn't smoke near her or at the apartment. She began to pace back and forth on the balcony and genuinely fearing for his safety he leaned back against the wall, unsure of what she might do. She slipped back in to the living room.

He slid to the ground and placed his hands in his face before wiping his mouth and searching for air in his lungs to speak words. Alcohol was still coursing through him and anxiety kept the words stuck in his chest.

She pulled out the plug from his record player, picked it up, and steamed towards the balcony. He tried to scramble to his feet but given that his equilibrium was out of whack, he fell back down and stared up pleadingly into her eyes as she paused before saying "STOP WASTING MY FUCKING TIME", before heaving the record player off the balcony. It spiraled downward, smashing on the asphalt. With an unchanged expression she returned to the living room and ripped the framed Fleetwood Mac LP from the wall and without even stepping back onto the balcony, frisbeed it through the opening and over the balcony's railing, before turning and storming away, slamming both the living room and bedroom doors. As he peered down into the car park at the fragments, his eye's welled-up and he began to gasp for air and felt sharp pains in his chest. When he finally got to his feet and re-entered, sliding the door shut, screams echoed from the bedroom. He lay down on the couch and his closing eyelids forced tears down his cheeks. The door swung open and she threw his jacket at him.

GET...THE FUCK... OUT...OF MY HOUSE...NOW!

*

He didn't know where he was going to go. As he walked up the ramp out of the complex, he realised he'd left his wallet behind but more importantly, he'd left his keys, again. He couldn't go back and there was no way he'd go near his parents' house.

*

After a minute of replaying what she'd said, she got up and went to the balcony in the hope that he'd still be in earshot. She could see him, almost at the gates, but he had his headphones on. The iPod, he never forgot.

Fucking asshole, where the hell is he even going to go?

The sun was fully up now. She starred at him walking up the road for a moment before her attention was drawn down to her ice-cold feet. She scanned the deck for cigarette butts but saw none. She couldn't smell any smoke either and sniffing the air, her eyes aligned with the bird feeder. Her chest began to cramp and her eyes welled-up as the penny dropped. She looked at what remained of the record player and the frame he'd gotten her and turned facing the empty space on the wall where the record had been.

Fuck.

*

With nowhere to go and no money he contemplated getting the Luas into town to seem refuge in the warmth of a Library but they wouldn't be open for another few hours. The idea of riding the Luas back and forth to stay warm reminded him of guys he'd seen in New York. He wasn't quite there yet. He ambled towards the empty playground. Sitting on a swing, he gripped the wet iron chains, leaned back and gazed up at the overcast sky. Leaning back further looking towards the trees, he noticed something hidden in the bushes. In the school bag he found a six-pack of Kepler's cider. Alongside the bag was a hurling stick that had been slid through an accompanying helmet. He'd kill some time before heading towards a friends' place to crash. After each can was finished he'd crush them under his boot into a puck before tossing them loftily into the air and batting them with the hurl over the monkey-bars, into the woods. He unzipped each pocket in search of potential smokes and or money for smokes but no joy. The last pocket however contained a naggin of Glen's Vodka. He finished it all off. Rage unbridled. Waves of things she'd said or not said, done and not done, were roaring in his mind. His heart was beating out of his chest and his breathing became laboured. He starred into a bleak pool of rippling rainwater beneath his swing. Soon it settled. He leaned over examining his pale face. His lower lip quivered and his eyes welled once more. He let out shaky yelp before grunting into a full-blown scream and dropping to his knees, began beating the murky water with clenched bloodless fists.

*

She had replaced the tossed LP with one of his she had rooted out of the crawl space under the stairs. Slayer, *Reign in Blood*. The sinister-looking black and blood-red vinyl cover had always unsettled her but now she smiled as she hung if from the wall, remembering the first time she went with him, reluctantly, to see them play in the Olympia Theatre. She'd feared being out of place and uncomfortable, imagining that the night would be torture as she'd be left alone while he moshed and head-banged the night away. But he didn't. He'd stuck to her all night and the only head-banging or heavy metal styled dancing he did was in-jest for her amusement, away from the wildness of the pit. The memory warmed her. She tilted the frame slightly knowing that he'd appreciate this symbolic middle-finger to conventionality. She thought of all they ways they were totally different, scanning the bookshelf; which books were hers and his were tragically obvious. *The Devil Wears Prada*, hers. *For Whom the Bell Tolls*, his. *Bridget Jones: The End of Reason,* hers. *As I Lay Dying*, his.

Bipolar for Dummies, hers. It had belonged to his parents but was given to her by his mother years ago. George the furry giraffe bookmark stared at her with his black-button eyes. He'd gotten her him as a gift. She sat down and opened the page that George was keeping for her. Also lodged between the pages was a pocked sized book called *The Little Book of Calm*, his.

Chapter 12: Lover Quarrels.

When a steamy romance morphs into a cauldron of conflict, the bipolar brain begins to boil and often seeks out conflict in order to feed its insatiable appetite for stimulation. Remaining cool when an episode occurs can be quite a challenge. In a manic or mixed episode your loved one may get right in your face and unleash a litany of abusive remarks and insults. Your initial impulse to lash back is like pouring kerosene on a blaze that's already out of control. Almost exaggerate your body language to show that you are actively listening intently. Let the rant run its natural course and when appropriate, phrase your statements and requests in non-confrontational language. YOU have the power to defuse the incident by simply allowing it to end. The more words you use, the more your loved one can attack back. Be thoughtful and let them know in no uncertain terms, that you love them. Do not stay silent. Non-responsiveness or an inability to express appropriate feelings can isolate your loved one and yield emotional meltdowns. Resolve conflicts immediately. Issues in the Bipolar Brain fester and

*build tension which eventually find a way of being expressed....prevent
an explosion. Couples therapy can often help you and your partner
develop the communication and problem solving skills you need to
keep disagreements from spinning out of control. SEE chapter 8 for
details.*

She had read this book soon after they'd first met and since forgotten
about it. In the years they'd been together he'd never had a major
episode like the ones she'd read about. Just as she finished reading
her highlighted paragraph she heard a thud at the door. This was
followed by another and another. She peered down the hall and
noticed cracks appearing around the hinges of the front door. One
more thud and it came crashing down.

Blood ran in splintered veins down the hurl. The hallway was
freezing and she could see his breath puffing out from behind the
bars of the hurling helmet. As he walked slowly across the door
saying nothing, he raised the hurl and dragged it along the wall,
knocking the pictures down one by one, leaving a long dripping red
streak. She stood frozen in her doorway. He stopped before her and
pointed the hurl.

BACK, THE FUCK...UP.

She stepped back into the living room and turned allowing him
pass. He stopped at the bookshelf before turning to face her.

SIT THE FUCK...DOWN.

I AM TAKING MY SHIT, AND I AM FUCKING GONE!

She sat down and let the silence linger before attempting to say the one and only word she could, and as her lips parted, he cut her off.

SHUT...THE FUCK...UP.

She knew what was about to happen and clutching George in her joined hands, felt a wave of calm come over her. She was not afraid.

The torrent of abuse began and without missing a beat for breath, he tore her character apart and fumed at her treatment of him. His main points of contention were his lack of sympathy for her chosen rat-race existence that she so-loathed and her crippling fear preventing her from doing anything to change it. He moved wildly about the room smashing every photo frame, overturning the bookcase, and sifted through a stack of records by his turn-tables, frisbeeing those that were hers across the room at her. He marched to the fridge and took out the bottle of wine with the label he'd made for their upcoming anniversary. He poured the contents down the drain and tossed the empty bottle onto the couch beside her.

MERRY FUCKING CHRISTMAS!

He then noticed his Slayer record on the wall. He rammed the butt of his hurl into the glass and he ripped the record out and removed it from its sleeve.

THAT'S FUCKING HILARIOUS...IMAGINE I GOT TO "ACTUALLY" LISTEN TO MY MUSIC OVER HERE... EVER...WELL GUESS WHAT? NOW'S THE TIME FOR ME TO EXIT IN A BLAZE OF FUCKING GLORY!

He put the record on one of the turntables, cranked the volume up, and let the needle down on the revolving wax. Before the music kicked-in he said, after noticing the book in her lap,

BIG FUCKING DEAL, YOU READ ONE BOOK AND YOU THINK YOU KNOW ME? YOU THINK YOU KNOW ME? YOU DON'T KNOW SHIT! AT LEAST I'M TRYING TO DO WHAT I WANT TO DO WITH MY FUCKING LIFE.

With that he picked up her stemless wineglass and finished the last drop, wild of eye, as *Angel of Death* kicked-in.

I HATE THESE STEMLESS FUCKING WINEGLASSES!

He lofted it into the air and swung for the fences. As the hurl connected, she felt as though time had slowed down. The glass exploded in the air and looked like spraying water.

She was, in this moment, transported to the instant she realised that she was in love with him and wanted to be with him for the rest of her life. They had been on a banana-boat while on a holiday in Turkey. She was sitting behind him with her arms and legs wrapped around him. Time had slowed down then too. He was running his fingertips through the water causing a refreshing spray. Sunlight glistened through the flying shards. His tattoos had bothered her a lot in the beginning of their relationship, especially when exposed on holidays, but in that moment, nothing else mattered. She loved him then just as she loved him in what she knew was only an episodic moment of madness.

His wild unblinking eyes should have scarred her as he frantically mouthed the lyrics while stamping around her living room in shattered glass, head-banging and screaming, but it didn't. He appeared to be tiring and as the song came to a close, he dropped the hurl and collapsed, exhausted, to the floor. His manic-fit had ended. He began to weep. She calmly stood up after a moment and removed the needle from the skipping record and lay down beside him on the bed of broken glass. She spooned into him, rocking and cooing. Neither of them said a word for several minutes. She waited for his breathing to return to normal, and his pounding heart to slow, before finally rolling him over and kissing the tears from his reddened cheeks and eyes, licking the saltiness. With a playful smile, she said. I love you...I'm sorry.

They held each other. Their attention turned to the sounds of a couple of wood pigeons cooing outside. They beheld the birdfeeder in all its glory. She squeezed his hand three times in-code (I-LOVE-YOU) acknowledging his thoughtfulness.

They sat back up together, leaning their backs against the couch. They watched, and listened and smiled. She pulled out a pack of cigarettes she'd hidden from under the couch. She drew out the last remaining for them to share and put it in his mouth before sparking it up. Staring down at their joined hands, they felt the sticky warmth of the blood joining them together.

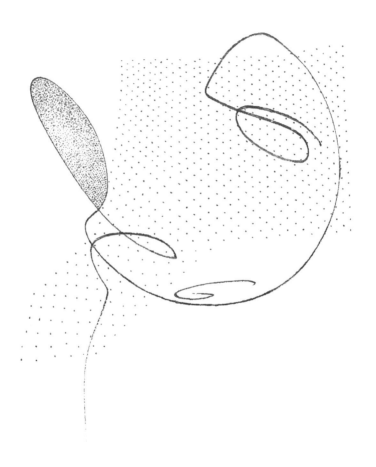

Urethral Valour

I derive undeniable pleasure in exercising a steady hand directing my stream, controlling the pressure of my release softly and evenly along the lip of the urinal, displacing an errant pube left by another without a drop hitting the floor or any spray defiling my jeans. The-then clean bowl can gleam pristine and is left inoffensive and welcoming for the next pissers-by.

I imagine the contents of their stomachs filled with undigested chunks of corn floating in processed beer and other waste their body has made of a burrito, which at least for that moment, can stay where it belongs and not be prompted upwards into their esophagus in response to the vile display of previous pisser's repugnant disregard for their fellow-man.

Even one person being spared, for me, is worth it. The prospect of those that I have offered this courtesy, going on to repeat the offense, does not unsettle me in the slightest as it would be puerile to be affected by that which is out of my control. We should all just try do our part, surely? My contempt for the guilty is only ever momentary. It is not a case of forgiving them, "for they know not what they do", as they are aware but simply do not care. This apathy, and I'm assuming in many cases, utter dejection, is a state of mind I am not wholly unsympathetic to, after all.

The satisfaction I gain in these instances, imagining the untroubled experience of those to use the urinal after me, is tantamount to that of the pube's journey itself. The human, so complex and capable, as we know, can be so fragile and violently arrested by the mere sight of an innocuous lone-hair. I feel better knowing someone wasn't put through that gutwrench, as I so often am.

I think of the pube itself, carried by the relief of many, through a labyrinth of pipes before being rebirthed into the Liffey. It will not sink. It will withstand its toxic environment, the elements and its isolation. It is not afraid. It is strong. It will not break or bruise. It will remain buoyant making its way to the sea where it can decompose in the calm.

The romantic notion of being reunited when my ashes are scattered is not entirely destroyed by my understanding of how long it will take the hair to disintegrate and the probability that I will outlive this. There are ships in the night. How truly different is any one hair from another?

I am safe in the knowledge, walking in the never-ending Dublin rain, that I am not in fact, alone. Somewhere there is someone, as we speak, employing the same attentiveness in guiding another marooned hair onto the path of its ultimate destination, the sea.

This will remain true when I am Dead and Gone, being scattered in the grey waves. Tonight, this revelation evokes a tear of joy or something of the sort, as I watch the hair spiral its way towards the drain. I hoped for the tear to plump enough to drop and be carried by the hair to her, but alas, it didn't make it in time.

It will follow though...they always do.

Gary Grace

About the Author

Gary Grace is a Writer from Dublin. He holds an honours degree in English Literature from Lesley University in Boston, Massachusetts. Gary primarily writes autobiographical fiction. He is an active member of the *Dublin Writers' Forum*, a volunteer at *Fighting Words* and in September 2019 will begin an MFA in Creative Writing at American College Dublin where he will be developing a collection of short stories and a novel. His short stories have been featured in *The Penny Dreadful, Word Legs* and *The Scum Gentry*.

www.gary-grace.com

garygrace10

Arizona Smith and Samuel Mead.

Collaboration

This book results from a collaboration between Gary Grace, the author and two artists, Arizona Smith and Samuel Mead. There are nine artworks in total, four each from Arizona and Sam and one - the first that appears in the book - a collaboration between both artists.

The purpose of the artwork was not necessarily to provide straightforward illustrations of scenes in the text, although in some cases the images take cues from the writing, but was focused on creating images that were inspired by the general mood and spirit of the stories - visual accompaniments rather than illustrations.

Arizona Smith and Samuel Mead are independent Artists who live and work in South London.

Their work can be viewed on Instagram **@arizonathecat** & @ **beg4cred** respectively.

Arizona also has a website arizonasmithart.com. Alternatively the artists can be reached via email, Arizonava@gmail.com and beg4cred@gmail.com.

Printed in Poland
by Amazon Fulfillment
Poland Sp. z o.o., Wrocław

At Night

GARY GRACE